A Summer Weekend

Adyasha Acharya

Ukiyoto Publishing

All global publishing rights are held by

Ukiyoto Publishing

Published in 2023

Content Copyright © Adyasha Acharya

ISBN 9789360163983

All rights reserved.
No part of this publication may be reproduced, transmitted, or stored in a retrieval system, in any form by any means, electronic, mechanical, photocopying, recording or otherwise, without the prior permission of the publisher.

The moral rights of the authors have been asserted.

This is a work of fiction. Names, characters, businesses, places, events, locales, and incidents are either the products of the author's imagination or used in a fictitious manner. Any resemblance to actual persons, living or dead, or actual events is purely coincidental.

This book is sold subject to the condition that it shall not by way of trade or otherwise, be lent, resold, hired out or otherwise circulated, without the publisher's prior consent, in any form of binding or cover other than that in which it is published.

www.ukiyoto.com

Dedicated to everyone who loves a good summer weekend.

Acknowledgement

I would like to thank my family and friends who have always supported my writing, be it good or bad.

A special thanks to my characters without whom I couldn't have done this.

And a huge thanks to Ukiyoto Publishing for giving me this great opportunity.

The thing I like most about summer is summer camps. I mean who can not like them. Games, activities, bonfire, barbecues and what not. And yes, of course swimming, boating and other water related activities.

This is the time when strangers be it kids or adults come together to have fun.

The bright golden sun rays streak my face as I move the wooden chairs in front of our Firefly Valley Lodge. The place gets its name from the fireflies that light up the sky during the nights every summer. It is beautiful and serene.

"Reese," my brother, Carter calls me from the porch of the lodge. He is holding two cartons of God knows what in his hands. I hadn't given him any list so what are these for. "Can you open the door for me?"

"Coming," I yell back.

Pulling the curtains apart, I hurry towards my brother to help him wondering where my parents are.

Mom is nowhere to be seen. She was in the garden a few minutes ago, tending to her precious poppies and roses. And Dad was supposed to be with Carter.

Our lodge is a three storeyed one with wooden exterior and a Vintage interior. It was designed by my grandfather himself. Dad has inherited the designer attributes from his father and is into carving.

Carter mutters a 'thank you' then places the boxes in the foyer.

"It is almost ten," he says shaking his head and his blonde hair. He has got his eyes and hair from our mother while mine is from our father. Honey brown strands and brown eyes.

I glance at the pendulum clock near the photograph wall at the side of the two-way stairs. The wall of photographs contains memories of our childhood till date. Of all the summer camps we have had since we were kids.

Five minutes to ten indeed. Meaning five minutes till the six kids show up for this weekend's summer camp.

Every week for two months we enrol five to six kids from age six to twelve from nearby towns and involve them in summer activities. It is so much fun. The kids love it. And so do I.

Straightening the hem of my pink top, I step out into the open to welcome this weekend's precious guests.

Summer camps are really exciting for me because I spend rest of my months with in the city working as an assistant editor. This is the only time I get to spend with my family.

I come home for the holidays but summers are my favorite since I was born on a hot summer night. My parents always say it is the reason why I love this season so much.

"Someone called for a singer," a captivating voice speaks up from the other end near the lake.

I jump down the steps to find Allen standing near his Ford with his arms crossed. He is dressed in a casual white button down shirt and a blue jeans and his dark brown hair is dishevelled.

"Oh my God!" I squeal in astonishment. Rushing over to him, I embrace him tightly. He plants a kiss to my forehead. "I thought you had to stay in town for two more days."

I am so excited to see him. I couldn't have imagined the weekend without him. Since the day we have met, he has always visited me on the summers at this lodge without fail.

"Well, it so happened that my favourite fan decided to attend a summer camp," he replies grinning. "I thought I would follow her."

"You lied." I smack his arm. "You told me you have to sign a new contract and had to stay back for two days otherwise we could have come together."

Allen smiles. That is a bad trick. And that gets me every single time. He and I have been dating for over two years now.

Allen is a fulltime singer and also gives music lessons at a high school near my publication house. That is how we met actually, one summer weekend.

"Are you going to invite me in or let me stand here as punishment, Sunshine?"

"You know I am not cruel. Come on in."

Allen follows me to the patio of our lodge. He already knows his way around here since he has been here with me twice previously. He also knows my parents and my brother.

"Are the kids here?" Mom calls from the garden, her face hidden away from the sun.

"Nope, Mom. Not those kids but another one whom you have known for two years."

Allen chuckles from behind me. The comparison is to the point.

Mom's honey gaze lands on us. She quickly hurries towards us and gives Allen a pat on the shoulders. "I am glad you came, son otherwise Reese's mood would have been spoiled."

"I couldn't have let that happen." Allen winks at me. Huh, charmer.

But Mom is right though. I would have missed Allen. He makes everything better.

The sound of tires forces us all to turn around. Dad's truck shows up in the driveway followed by three cars. The kids are here.

Mom wipes her hands on her apron then removes it and throws it on the white wooden chair in our lawn. Carter comes outside holding out two cowboy hats. He must have heard Allen's voice and realized that he is here.

He hands them to both of us. "Thought you might need them."

"Thanks," I say handing over one to Allen.

Carter and Allen shake hands. "Glad to see you here, dude."

"Glad to be here," Allen replies grinning.

Dad gets out of his truck. The kids and their parents do the same. Five of them this time. Two girls and three boys. The girls- Leila and Kristy are 10 and 7 years old. And the boys - Ken, Noah and Han are 8, 12 and 6.

"Welcome everyone!" I wave at the kids. All five of them wave back enthusiastically.

Dad beckons Mom over to talk to the parents of the kids. The parents would need reassurance that the kids will be safe here. And it is our duty to provide them so.

We are also responsible for the safey and well being of the kids since they would be staying away from their parents and homes be it for a weekend.

Carter joins them leaving Allen and me with the kids.

Noah, who has been with us once previously along with his sister Kristy, glances at Allen. "Who is he?" Allen hadn't been here with us that time.

I wonder how to tell him he is my boyfriend in front of the rest of them so I am about to say my best friend when Allen speaks up. "The Prince Charming of course."

"You are the Prince Charming from Cinderella?" Kristy's eyes gleam with wonder.

"No, no not from Cinderella." Allen tips his hat down. "I am from the other side of the world. There is a mysterious city where I live. The city has flying carpets and magicians."

I laugh having pictured Allen on a white horse wearing a crown and rushing through the woods. I thought he was going to say something like that. But I guess he likes urban fantasies.

"Who is the princess then?" Ken asks.

Ah yes, I would like to know that too. I raise a brow at Allen.

"Why, this beautiful lady here of course!" Allen nudges my shoulder and my cheeks turn red.

Before he can say anything else, I take the initiative.

"Okays, guys! Let me show you around the lodge and your rooms."

The tour consists of me actually showing them around with Allen throwing funny comments and us bickering. In the end, I am annoyed, Allen satisfied and the kids happy having enjoyed us arguing.

The dorm room consists of ten beds. But for this weekend five shall be occupied. Mom and Dad sleep on the room across while Carter at the end of the hall.

My room is on the first floor along with two guest rooms. One is reserved for when Allen comes here. He has few of his spare things and clothes already kept here.

The second floor has the library and the activity room consisting of various instruments, art and craft materials and a big flat screen.

The rooftop has a pool and various decorative plants.

"You all will be sleeping here," I say opening the door to the dorm room. "Boys to the left and girls to my right."

"Yes, captain," Allen immediately responds saluting at me.

I glare at him. "I wasn't referring to you."

"You said in the morning that you consider me a kid yourself." He grins at me.

Right. Shouldn't have had forgotten that I said that because Allen doesn't forget a thing I do or say.

"You maybe a kid but you won't fit on any of these beds," I counterreact.

There is no way I am letting him win this time. He has already been teasing me throughtout the whole lodge tour.

The kids start to snicker. Ha! Reese: 1, Allen: 0.

He leans forward and my breath stops. He wouldn't do this in front of all these kids right? Would he now?

"Laters, Sunshine."

I bite my cheek, my face red from his action. God, he is such a melodramatic guy. But he is mine.

"Kids, don't you think you should call Sunshine here captain. She walks and talks like one."

I pout at him. "And what are you then?"

"The First Mate." Quite obvious.

"I wouldn't give you such an important position on my ship."

"I think you would. You have already."

The kids look confused. Yeah, I bet we don't know what we are talking about either.

I ignore him, conveniently this time. "Lunch will be served in the dining room downstairs in two hours."

There is still time left so I need to come up with something so that they don't get bored. "Now, who wants to watch a movie?"

Taking the kids to the activity room, I switch on the flat screen and play Narnia. It was one of my favourite movies when I had been a kid. I bet these kids will love it too.

Time passes by as we all lounge together on the couch and watch the movie attentively. In between at times, Allen pokes his finger on my shoulder to disturb me. I smack his arm to make him stop.

He tugs on my arm to get a moment alone with him so I follow him into the hallway.

"You can't sit idle for some time right?" I accuse him.

"Of course not. I love the kids but I love you more so when am I going to get some time with you."

I loop my arms around his neck. "I stay with you throughout the year, remember?"

"That's there. This is here."

He is so cute sometimes. "Aww." I plant a kiss to the tip of his nose.

"Reese," Kristy calls me from inside. "Allen. The climax scene is here."

Mom shows up some time later with seven big glasses of mango and orange juices. The mangoes and oranges are grown in our orchard itself.

"Tasty," Han says licking his lips.

"Here," I pick up a tissue to wipe his mouth clean. "Do you want more?"

"Yes!" all the kids say in unison.

The movie ends then we head downstairs to the dining room. Lunch consists of spaghetti, meatballs, prawns and pudding as dessert.

My parents are experts in cooking. Carter is pathetic and I somehow manage to make something decent. Though not that good. At least not that bad.

"You guys are great cooks," Allen compliments my parents. "Everytime I come here, I feel as if I am in heaven."

"Too bad I can't cook this well," I grumble taking a bite of my pudding.

"Your sweet voice and pure soul makes up for that," he says grinning.

I almost choke on my pudding. "Allen."

"What?"

"You can be a little more subtle."

"That was subtle and you know it."

"Allen never misses a chance to praise you," Dad teases me. Dad and Mom say they'll clean the dishes and send us upstairs with the kids. The kids being tired go to the dorm room for a nap.

Carter and I go to the living room to talk while Allen does his unpacking. We talk about my recent projects, his law firm the one which our family owns aside from the lodge. About our grandparents and how happy they'd have been to know that this lodge has become so popular.

"You didn't invite Jenna this time?" I ask him.

Jenna is Carter's girlfriend and he seemed serious regarding her. Or maybe there is some trouble in paradise.

"She wanted to come but it is her sister's baby shower tomorrow."

Atleast they aren't having any relationship issues. I would have hated it because I like Jenna and she really cares for my brother.

"You should go over to her's after this weekend is over."

"Yeah, I am planning on it."

He gives me a crooked smile. "What?" I spread my arms in question.

"Allen and you seem to be growing stronger together every time I see you two."

"It is because we have been together for two years. Time has an effect, you know."

"Have you thought of getting married? Has he asked you?"

"You think he wouldn't talk to you before asking me or that he would ask me and I wouldn't tell you guys."

I bet he is waiting for a perfect day. But he knows that if he would pop up that question I would say yes in a heartbeat.

Carter and I chat for a bit more then head to our rooms.

At five o' clock, I wake the kids up and we have a quick snack then head over for boating. Carter, me, Allen and two kids with us while Mom, Dad and the others on another boat.

I click a lot of pictures. Allen splashes water on me from the lake and all of us in our boat end up wet eventually.

"You weren't this mischievous when you were a kid," I remark.

"Nope," he agrees grinning.

His mom had told me when I had gone to his house the very first time that he was like a regular kid, always spending time on the playground or in his Dad's music studio.

"How people change!" I drawl.

He chuckles. "You weren't this melodramatic when you were a kid I bet."

"No, she was actually," Carter answers for me.

"Liar," I mutter.

"I guess for this once I would like to believe Carter."

"Traitor," I comment at Allen who throws his head back and laughs.

We eventually get off the boat and I give the kids each a towel to dry off. I wouldn't want them to catch a cold and go home sneezing.

During the night, we enjoy a swim in our pool only for fifteen minutes because half of them had already gotten wet while on the boat.

Carter then teaches them origami.

"That's my paper," Kristy yells at Han.

"No mine," Leila interrupts.

They start to quarrel among themselves and throw the papers around.

"Wow, this is a battleground now," Allen mumbles from the couch.

Carter glances at me for assistance. "Help, sis."

"Kids!" I shout.

No one listens to me.

"Again," Allen nudges me.

"You first shut up," I glare at him.

He puts a finger to his mouth and nods, that smirk still on his face.

"Okay, guys, if you don't stop quarelling right now, I am gonna have to cancel all your activities for tomorrow, call your parents and send you all back home."

All the kids fall silent in just two seconds.

"Finally," Carter mutters wiping his forehead. "Good job, sis."

"Thanks."

"Proud of you, Sunshine," Allen adds.

"Yes, I was waiting for your compliment."

He chuckles. "I know, right."

The origami session finally gets over with the kids having made various paper figurines of different colours.

Then we head downstairs to the dining hall for dinner.

"Everyone, listen up!" Dad announces while dinner.

I curiously turn to him along with the others. "Tomorrow morning, we have a surprise for you all!"

I wonder what surprise it is because even I don't know. And from Carter's and Allen's faces, I bet they don't know either.

Only my parents know about it. They must have planned an activity.

The kids start babbling about what the surprise might be.

Mom clicks the spoon on the table. "But for that you'll have to wake up a little early. We promise it will be fun."

After dinner, Mom and Dad take the kids to the dorm room to tuck them into bed.

Carter heads over to his room to have a video chat with Jenna.

Yawning, I walk upstairs to my room trailed by Allen. "Hey, Sunshine?"

"Yes?"

His green eyes study me for a moment. "I am writing a new song."

"Wow!" We reach my bedroom door. Allen lingers in the hallway not wanting to leave. "What is it about?"

Allen writes his own songs and all of them are so beautiful and heart touching. His lyrics and his voice are something worth admiration.

"That is a surprise. I'll tell you tomorrow."

"That makes two surprises for tomorrow."

"Both will be good."

"I am positive about your song but I am not quite sure about what my parents have planned for the kids and us."

Allen laughs, his eyes sparkling. "You really have a way of saying things."

"Isn't that why you fell in love with me?"

"Yeah, absolutely. One of many more things."

"There are more," I cover my mouth with my hand melodramatically. "Care to share?"

"No, I would like you to make more efforts and find out yourself."

"Cruel."

"I am wounded." He kisses me goodnight. "I'll see you when the sun shines. Good night, Reese."

"Good night, Allen."

....

I get up early in the morning as instructed by my parents and take a quick shower. Getting dressed in a pair of denims and a peach top, I go to the kitchen to have a cereal breakfast.

Mom must have taken breakfast for the kids to have in their dorm room and be helping them to get ready.

I quickly finish my breakfast and head to the dorm room where the kids are busy getting ready.

The men of the house are all missing. They must be outside. I hope Dad doesn't share the secret with them then everyone will know everything except the kids and me.

"Ready guys?" I ask the kids.

"Yesss!" they respond in chorus.

"Let's go outside then."

Dad, Allen and Carter are indulged in a hearty conversation when we reach outside.

"Wat is so funny?" Mom inquires smiling.

"Just boy talks," Dad replies laughing.

"None of you is a boy," I retort rolling my eyes.

Carter huffs. "She always says that but we are younger at heart than her."

"Ignored," I wave him off. "So, what is the surprise you guys were talking about yesterday at dinner?" I ask putting on my hat.

"We are going on a scavenger hunt!" Dad replies enthusiastically.

"Yay!" The kids shout exuberantly.

"I have hidden a box full of fireworks in the woods behind us. You'll be divided into teams and the one who finds the box first wins."

He puts his hands on his hips. "Team A is Reese, Allen, Noah and Kristy and B is Carter, Ken, Han, Leila. You have two hours."

That is too much of time. Where exactly has Dad hidden the box?

"Lunch will be ready by the time you guys get back," Mom adds.

"Let's do this!" Carter says lifting a fist in the air then stops short. "But Dad, the clue?"

Everyone laughs. I mean of course where would have we gone without the clue?

"Yeah, right. The clue. The answer is in the middle of where gravity started and the water source ended."

What kind of weird clue is that now? Dad does have a knack for riddles.

Allen raises his brow. "Gravity started?"

"That is just for rhyming purpose," I reply shrugging. "But it must be related to gravity though."

Noah and Kristy follow us as we trudge through the woods. Ravens fly overhead, their shadows dancing across our faces. A light breeze flows caressing our cheeks.

"Could it be related to a place with good height?" Allen suggests. "Gravity is more there, right?"

"Is it related to apples?" Noah says from behind me. "Newton first discovered gravity when he was sitting under an apple tree."

Could be. "We have few apple trees at the end of our farm."

"And the water source?" Kristy asks sweetly.

"The lake goes around the farm and ends there. It must mean the box is somewhere there."

That would be a good place to hide a box. Plus Dad wouldn't really hide it somewhere so difficult that we won't ever find it.

Allen starts running and we tail behind. The path is curved but clear. We finally reach the end of the farm. Carter and his team aren't here yet.

We are leading then.

"The lake ends there," Allen points at the small bridge that goes into the woods and the turning that marks the end of the road too.

"The apple trees," Kristy motions at the three huge apple trees near the fence.

"There," I say walking towards a small red x marked near the bridge.

The four of us quickly dig up the earth to reveal a brown coloured box. "We found it," Noah claps.

Kristy hugs her brother. "We won."

Carter and his team just arrive as we pull the box out. "Ah, man!" Carter sighs.

"Don't worry, we'll all get to see the fireworks," I reassure him.

"That is right though."

....

Dad and Carter make us a bonfire while Allen and I set the chairs. The kids help Mom set the barbecue on the white table near the lake.

"All done," Dad lights the bonfire.

Carter opens the box and lights a firecracker. The golden light shines on our faces. The kids stare at it in awe and exuberance.

"It is really beautiful," I whisper sitting beside Allen.

"Yes, like you."

"You don't miss any moment to compliment me," I smile at him.

He grins. "Of course not. That would be a blunder."

"Barbecue's ready," Mom announces from a few feet away near the grill stand.

The aroma of delicious grilled barbecue fills my nose.

"I have to say your Mom is a Masterchef," Allen confesses.

"That she is."

Allen and I help Mom serve the food while Dad and Carter keep lighting up the fireworks.

Then we all sit down on the carpet and enjoy the delicious barbecue grilled by Mom.

Once we are finished with the food, Allen stands up. "It is time for my surprise, Sunshine," he whispers to me then disappears inside the lodge.

He returns with his guitar. "I have written a new song and I'd like to share it with you all."

He starts playing an acoustic tune on his guitar. *"When the sun goes out, I'll be around, you'll never be alone, never be alone...."* His melodious voice fills the surroundings. *"I'll walk with you, every step, every road, hmmmm...."*

"Who is it for?" Leila asks after the song is over and we applaud.

"Why, of course it is for the princess I was telling you about." He glances at me. "The one I met on a summer weekend."

****

About the Author

Adyasha Acharya

Dr. Adyasha Acharya is a medical intern in Bhubaneswar, Odisha, India. She is a voracious reader and her most favourite genres are fantasy and science fiction. She has published two novels previously- "The Fearless Warriors" (2015) and "The Guardian" (2021), a short story titled "Nexus" and "The Psychics" in the Indian Periodical Magazine and "The Midnight Ritual" in the anthology "The Selection of a Sacred Strawberry" by Writefluence (2023).

www.ingramcontent.com/pod-product-compliance
Lightning Source LLC
LaVergne TN
LVHW041602070526
838199LV00046B/2099